HAIL, HAIL, HOLLENHEAD'S HERE!

Whether Danny Hollenhead and his chums are exorcising haunted dorm radiators, skewering jock festival rites, or donating complaining corpuscles to the blood drive, cartoon creator Sabin C. Streeter earns top honors as the cartoonist to a new generation. His wild and witty observations capture the never-ending absurdities of academia in a hilarious blend of the real and the ridiculous. It makes college almost as much fun as kindergarten.

SABIN C. STREETER is a junior at Yale University, where he has drawn *Hollenhead* for two years for the *Yale Daily News*.

To my brothers,
Gordon and George

my first editors,
Lisa, Crocker, Henry and Aaron

and my friends, especially
Chad, Matthew, Francis and Gillian

HOLLENHEAD

Sabin C. Streeter

A PLUME BOOK
NAL PENGUIN INC.
NEW YORK AND SCARBOROUGH, ONTARIO

NAL PENGUIN BOOKS ARE AVAILABLE AT QUANTITY DISCOUNTS WHEN USED TO PROMOTE PRODUCTS OR SERVICES. FOR INFORMATION PLEASE WRITE TO PREMIUM MARKETING DIVISION, NAL PENGUIN INC., 1633 BROADWAY, NEW YORK, NEW YORK 10019.

Copyright © 1987 by Sabin C. Streeter

All rights reserved

 PLUME TRADEMARK REG. U.S. PAT. OFF. AND FOREIGN COUNTRIES
REGISTERED TRADEMARK—MARCA REGISTRADA
HECHO EN SECAUCUS, N.J., U.S.A.

SIGNET, SIGNET CLASSIC, MENTOR, ONYX, PLUME, MERIDIAN and NAL BOOKS are published *in the United States* by NAL Penguin Inc., 1633 Broadway, New York, New York 10019, and *in Canada* by The New American Library of Canada Limited, 81 Mack Avenue, Scarborough, Ontario M1L 1M8

Library of Congress Cataloging-in-Publication Data

Streeter, Sabin C.
  Hollenhead.

  I. Title.
PN6728.H6S7 1987   741.5'973   86-33140
ISBN 0-452-25954-1

First Printing, March, 1987

1 2 3 4 5 6 7 8 9

PRINTED IN THE UNITED STATES OF AMERICA

UM - I'M FROM ACROSS THE HALL AND I THINK THERE'S A CULT CEREMONY GOING ON IN THERE. DO YOU KNOW ANYTHING ABOUT IT?
THREE BUCKS, DUDE.
10-29-85
BEER! PARTY!
GIMME THREE BUCKS AND I'LL STAMP YOUR HAND; THEN YOU CAN JOIN THE PARTY AND DRINK BEER.
WHAT?!
I KNEW IT! IT'S A CULT! FIRST THEY WANT MONEY, THEN THEY WANT YOU TO EAT FLOWERS AND CHANT ZIP CODES! WELL, YOU WON'T GET A CENT FROM ME!
OKAY KID, FORGET THE MONEY! I'LL JUST STAMP YOU—
HEY DAVE — WHAT'S ALL THE NOISE?!
AAAYYY! I'VE BEEN MARKED! I'M DOOMED! I'M DOOMED!
I DON'T KNOW WHAT HIS PROBLEM IS, HE JUST WON'T STOP YELLING. MAYBE HE DOESN'T LIKE BEER.
NO WAY! DID YOU TELL HIM IT'S SCHAEFER?

34

HEY LIZ, I GOT YOU A BEER.
OOOO! ANOTHER ONE FOR ME?
I WOULDN'T TAKE THAT IF I WERE YOU.
10-31-85
WHAT?!
WHY NOT?
BECAUSE HE JUST WANTS TO FATTEN YOU UP BEFORE THEY SACRIFICE YOU.
HEY! WATCH YOUR MOUTH!
SEE, AFTER THEY STOP WORSHIPPING THAT METAL CYLINDER, THEY'LL WANT SOMEONE TO TIE TO A STAKE AND SACRIFICE—THAT'S HOW ALL CULT RITUALS END!
WOW-I'D NEVER THOUGHT OF IT THAT WAY BEFORE!

ZZZMMPH... HUH?! WHERE AM I?! WHAT'S GOING ON?! ...SOMEBODY GET ME A BEER!
I'M AFRAID THAT'S IMPOSSIBLE, THE CEREMONY IS OVER - YOUR GOD DIED AND EVERYONE WENT HOME.
11-1-85
SO WHAT IF THE KEG'S BEAT?! THERE MUST BE A BEER HERE SOMEWHERE - GO FIND IT! I NEED A BEER!
OK-OK-UM-NO PROBLEM! UM-AH-AH-HEY! I FOUND ONE!
GIVE IT TO ME! BRING IT HERE!
THERE YOU GO - IT WAS IN YOUR ROOM.
OHH! A BEER! A BEER! A BEER! OHHHHH! BEER! BEER! BEER! BEER! BEER! BEER!
I DON'T HAVE THE HEART TO TELL HIM IT'S HIS DEODORANT.

AH, EXCUSE ME, ARE YOU LOOKING FOR SOMETHING?
WELL-YEAH, I'M THE BUILDING INSPECTOR AND WE'RE LOOKING FOR THE TIMOTHY DWIGHT DORMITORY BUILDING.
11-19-85
OH, IT'S RIGHT OVER THERE - THEY'LL BE GLAD TO SEE YOU, TOO! I'VE HEARD THE CEILINGS ARE CRUMBLING AND PLASTER HAS BEEN FALLING LIKE CRAZY! UM-SAY, WHO'S YOUR FRIEND?
I'M THE BUILDING EXORCIST.
GULP- EXORCIST?! BUT I THOUGHT IT WAS JUST A LEAKY ROOF—
APPARENTLY NOT.
HEY CHRIS! IT'S HAPPENING AGAIN!
GRRRR- GET OUT!

38

39

OK, I'VE THROWN IN THE HOLY NAILS AND READ THE MEDIEVAL ARCHITECTURE CHANTS – NOW ALL WE CAN DO IS WAIT...
EXORCISM MADE EASY
11-22-85
POOF!
WOW! IT'S EMPTY!! WHAT HAPPENED?
THE EXORCISM IS OVER. ACCORDING TO EXORCIST TRADITION, SATAN HAS LEFT THE DORM AND GONE BACK TO HELL.
ACTUALLY, I'M TRANSFERRING TO THE LAW SCHOOL.

41

ANDY, I'M SORRY, BUT I CAN'T GIVE YOU A DEAN'S EXCUSE JUST BECAUSE YOU DIDN'T DO ANY WORK OVER BREAK. YOU HAVE TO HAVE A REASON—
I WAS VERY BUSY.
12-3-85
DOING WHAT?
RESEARCH! HERE, LOOK AT MY REPORT—
HMM... TEN PAGES ON THE COMPARATIVE VALUES OF BORDEN AND SEALTEST EGGNOG.
I'VE EVALUATED THEM FOR RICHNESS, CREAMINESS, REAL EGGY FLAVOR, AND NUTMEG CONTENT—
I TAKE IT YOU'RE PLEADING INSANITY?
PERHAPS YOU'D LIKE TO SEE MY ANALYSIS OF THE YODEL—
EARNS

43

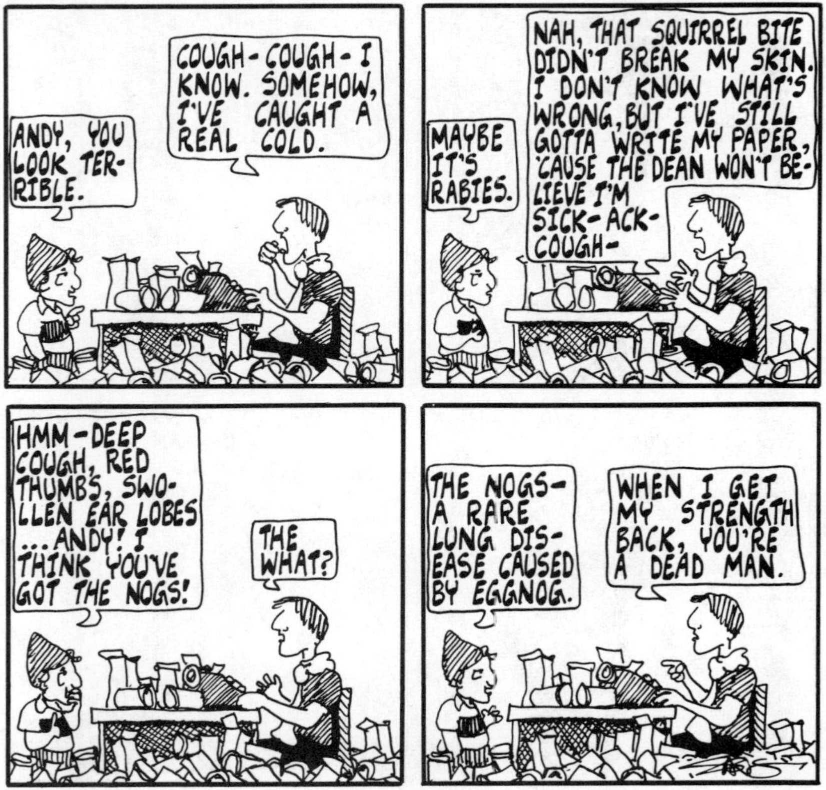
ANDY, YOU LOOK TER-RIBLE.
COUGH-COUGH-I KNOW. SOMEHOW, I'VE CAUGHT A REAL COLD.
MAYBE IT'S RABIES.
NAH, THAT SQUIRREL BITE DIDN'T BREAK MY SKIN. I DON'T KNOW WHAT'S WRONG, BUT I'VE STILL GOTTA WRITE MY PAPER, 'CAUSE THE DEAN WON'T BE-LIEVE I'M SICK-ACK-COUGH-
HMM-DEEP COUGH, RED THUMBS, SWO-LLEN EAR LOBES ...ANDY! I THINK YOU'VE GOT THE NOGS!
THE WHAT?
THE NOGS-A RARE LUNG DIS-EASE CAUSED BY EGGNOG.
WHEN I GET MY STRENGTH BACK, YOU'RE A DEAD MAN.

ACK-ACK-ACK-COUGH-COUGH-I'M DEAD; I'M TOO SICK TO STAY AWAKE, AND I'VE GOTTA WRITE A PAPER ON MOSS BY TOMORROW, AND THE DEAN WON'T GIVE ME AN EXCUSE BECAUSE I NEEDED SIX OF THEM LAST SEMESTER—
9-26-86
WHEEZE - WHEEZE I'LL NEVER GET IT DONE - I'M GOING TO FAIL - NOTHING CAN SAVE ME - I'M DOOMED—
Z-Z-Z
HI, WE'RE ELVES!
SHUT UP, FOOLS! HE'S NOT SUPPOSED TO KNOW!
WE'LL WRITE YOUR PAPER!

Z-Z-Z-H-HMMPH! HUH? WHAT'S THIS? —OH — IT'S MY PAPER: "MOSS, BY ANDREW PARSLEY" ... WAIT A MINUTE. I'VE BEEN ASLEEP!— WHO WROTE THIS?!
WE DID!
2-27-86
YOU? WHO ARE YOU?
WE'RE ELVES. WE WROTE YOUR PAPER BECAUSE YOU WERE TOO SICK TO DO IT.
WELL, THANKS A LOT! I REALLY APPRECIATE IT! I — HEY! YOU COPIED THIS OUT OF THE ENCYCLOPEDIA!
WE DIDN'T KNOW ANYTHING ABOUT MOSS.
THIS IS USELESS! I CAN'T HAND THIS IN!
WE'RE SORRY.
WE DID OUR BEST.
MAYBE WE COULD FIX YOUR SHOES INSTEAD.

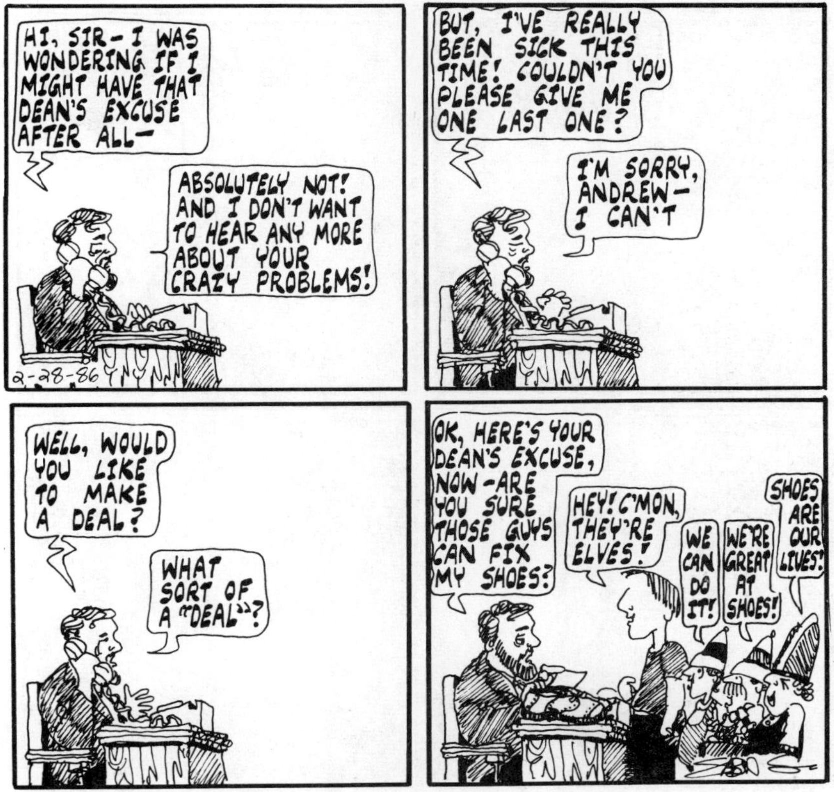
HI, SIR– I WAS WONDERING IF I MIGHT HAVE THAT DEAN'S EXCUSE AFTER ALL–
ABSOLUTELY NOT! AND I DON'T WANT TO HEAR ANY MORE ABOUT YOUR CRAZY PROBLEMS!
2-28-86
BUT, I'VE REALLY BEEN SICK THIS TIME! COULDN'T YOU PLEASE GIVE ME ONE LAST ONE?
I'M SORRY, ANDREW– I CAN'T
WELL, WOULD YOU LIKE TO MAKE A DEAL?
WHAT SORT OF A "DEAL"?
OK, HERE'S YOUR DEAN'S EXCUSE, NOW–ARE YOU SURE THOSE GUYS CAN FIX MY SHOES?
HEY! C'MON, THEY'RE ELVES!
WE CAN DO IT!
WE'RE GREAT AT SHOES!
SHOES ARE OUR LIVES!

ELKMAN NEEDS A HOBBY TO SUSTAIN HIM IN HIS OLD AGE.
TAXIDERMY
SAWDUST
REMEMBER WHEN ELKMAN BOUGHT THE KELP AND DECIDED TO BECOME A TAXIDERMIST?
KELP
TAXIDERMY
SAWDUST
TAXIDERMY IS AN ANCIENT AND REVERED ART; KELP ARE ANCIENT AND REVERED SEA CREATURES-
KELP
SAWDUST
TAXIDERMY
NONETHELESS ELKMAN, YOU CAN'T STUFF KELP! THEY DON'T HAVE MOUTHS!
REMEMBER WHEN ELKMAN'S NEW HOBBY WAS DISMISSED BY THE SKEPTICS?
SAWDUST
TAXIDERMY

49

REMEMBER WHEN ELKMAN LEARNED THE RECIPE FOR KELP JAM?
C'MON ELK-MAN, DON'T YOU WANT TO STUFF THIS WOLF?
R-R-R
SUGAR
JAM
10-29-86
FIRST, ELKMAN PUT HALF A POUND OF KELP, TWO POUNDS OF SUGAR, FOUR TEASPOONS OF PECTIN, AND ONE GALLON OF KEROSENE IN THE BOILER.
FINE, SUIT YOURSELF.
THEN, ELKMAN SET THE BOIL-ER TO FIVE HUNDRED DE-GREES.
REMEMBER WHEN ELKMAN LEARNED THAT KEROSENE WASN'T AN INGREDIENT IN KELP JAM?
BOOM!
YOU SHOULD HAVE STUCK WITH TAXI-DERMY.

HELLO?
HEY, ELKMAN'S HERE WITH THE KELP JAM!
JAM $5
10-30-86
"KELP JAM"?
REMEMBER WHEN ELKMAN HAD ALL THAT KELP AND DECIDED TO MAKE JAM AND SELL IT DOOR TO DOOR?
JAM $5
YOU'RE SELLING THIS STUFF?
HEY, OLD ELKMAN'S GOTTA MAKE A LIVING.
JAM $5
I'LL BET IT TASTES AWFUL.
REMEMBER WHEN ELKMAN OFFERED A FREE JUG OF KELP SYRUP WITH EVERY PURCHASE?
AND DON'T FORGET THE COMPLIMENTARY STUFFED WOLF!
JAM $5

WHAT THE HELL IS THIS, KATE?
A STUFFED WOLF.
10-31-86
WHAT'S IT DOING HERE?
OH, THESE GUYS CAME BY SELLING KELP JAM FOR FIVE DOLLARS A JAR, SO I BOUGHT ONE AND GOT IT FOR FREE.
YOU'RE KIDDING!
I FELT SORRY FOR THEM. YOU KNOW HOW HARD IT IS TO GET RID OF KELP THESE DAYS. BESIDES, IT'S A NICE WOLF.
HEY, REMEMBER WHEN ELKMAN USED THE REST OF THE KELP TO MAKE A QUILT?
LOCK THE DOOR!

HI, I'M THE CARTOONIST WHO DRAWS THIS STRIP, SPEAKING TO YOU AS A CAN OF SPAM. BEHIND ME ARE KEVIN AND DOUG. CHRISTMAS VACATION IS OVER AND THEY'RE READY FOR THE FIRST DAY OF CLASSES IN THE NEW SEMESTER. ORDINARILY, THIS IS CONSIDERED TO BE A RATHER BORING DAY...
SPAM
9-3-86
HEY DOUG! WELCOME BACK! ARE YOU READY FOR CLASSES?
SURE AM, KEVIN!
ONLY THIS IS NOT GOING TO BE AN ORDINARY FIRST DAY FOR KEVIN— HE'S ABOUT TO BE CRUSHED BY A FALLING TRUNK...
SPAM
CRASH
WHOA!
DOUG THINKS HE'S BEEN LUCKY, BUT HE DOESN'T KNOW THAT THIS ISN'T GONNA BE AN ORDINARY FIRST DAY FOR HIM EITHER— HE'S ABOUT TO BE RUN DOWN BY A CO-OP VAN...
SPAM
HAPPY FIRST DAY, DOUG.
AYY!
CO-OP
VROOM
HAVE A NICE FIRST DAY OF CLASSES, EVERYONE...
SPAM

1-15-85
I CAN'T BELIEVE I'M DOING THIS AGAIN — EVERY SEMESTER THEY MAKE ME TEACH THIS GUT TO DOPES WHO NEED A SCIENCE CLASS! ... LOOK AT 'EM — NOT ONE COULD CARE LESS! AND I'M A FULL-FLEDGED PROFESSOR AND A RESPECTED MEMBER OF THE SCIENTIFIC COMMUNITY!! —
WELL, KIDS, I'VE GOT A SURPRISE FOR YOU — I'M SICK OF YOUR SLEEPING; NOT DOING THE READINGS OR PROBLEM SETS; AND NOT GOING TO SECTIONS! THIS SEMESTER YOU'RE GOING TO SHOW SOME INTEREST! THIS SEMESTER THINGS ARE GONNA BE DIFFERENT!
AH, EXCUSE ME — AH COULD I HAVE SOME QUIET, PLEASE?
I SAID, QUIET!
ZAP-ZAP
AYYY!
THIS SEMESTER I'M BRINGING MY DEATH-RAY.

HELLO, AND WELCOME TO "ASTRONOMY 97B: AN INTRODUCTION TO ASTROPHYSICS FOR THE SCIENTIFICALLY UNINTERESTED". THE COURSE TEXTBOOK WILL AGAIN BE, "OUR FRIEND THE UNIVERSE", NOW ON SALE AT THE BOOKSTORE.—
1-16-86
—BUT, THIS SEMESTER I'VE DECIDED TO DO A MORE IN-DEPTH EXAMINATION OF THE HISTORY OF ASTRONOMY, AND ON THE SYLLABUS, YOU'LL SEE THAT I'VE ASSIGNED SOME OF THE ORIGINAL WRITINGS OF COPERNICUS AND KEPLER. I EXPECT—
—AH—EXCUSE ME, SIR?
YES?
AH—I'M SORRY, SIR—BUT IF I REMEMBER CORRECTLY, THOSE BOOKS HAVE BEEN OUT OF PRINT FOR OVER THREE HUNDRED YEARS.
YEAH? AND THEY'RE ALSO IN MEDIEVAL LATIN.—YOU GOT A PROBLEM?
UM—NO SIR! I LOVE THAT STUFF!

OK, I THOUGHT I'D SHOW SOME SLIDES AS A BRIEF INTRODUCTION: HERE IS OUR UNIVERSE, NOTICE THE BIG, WHITE BALL IN THE CENTER. THAT'S OUR SUN, IT'S VERY HOT AND VERY BRIGHT.
CLICK
HMMM
HMM
1-7-86
THIS NEXT SLIDE IS A DETAIL OF THE SUN, NOTICE THE LITTLE SURFACE BUMPS. THESE ARE CHEMICAL EXPLOSIONS WHICH CONTINUOUSLY OCCUR IN THE SUN, PRODUCING ALL THAT HEAT AND LIGHT-
CLICK
YAWN
HMMM
YAWN
NOW, THIS IS THE SAME SLIDE, MAGNIFIED 600 TIMES BY A PROCESS I DESIGNED. IT REPRESENTS THE SUN AS IF IT WERE SEEN FROM MERCURY AND ONLY SLIGHTLY DAMAGES THE HUMAN EYE.
CLICK
YOW!
HA-HA-HA! PRETTY BRIGHT, EH? HERE'S HALLEY'S COMET, MAGNIFIED TO APPEAR THIRTY YARDS AWAY-
CLICK
AYYY!

YOU KNOW, WE'VE GOTTA DECLARE OUR MAJORS AND GET A FACULTY ADVISOR THIS WEEK.
DON'T REMIND ME.
1-20-86
I'M THINKING ABOUT DOING ECONOMICS, HOW 'BOUT YOU?
I'M NOT SURE- I KEEP THINKING I SHOULD GO FOR MATH. IT'S GOT A GOOD BALANCE BETWEEN THEORY AND APPLICATION
STILL, IF I COULD GET MY ACT TOGETHER, I'D LIKE TO TRY HISTORY. IT'S MORE INTERESTING TO ME THAN MATH AND I THINK A SENIOR ESSAY WOULD BE A GREAT CHALLENGE.
WOW, THAT'S A PRETTY TOUGH CHOICE-
YEAH, I'LL PROBABLY JUST DO FORESTRY.

MOM, DAD — HI! I JUST CALLED TO SAY I'VE DECIDED TO MAJOR IN FORESTRY.
HAVE YOU LOST YOUR MIND?!
THAT'S NICE, DEAR.
1-21-86
YALE HAS A BIG FOREST ESTATE, SO I'LL BE ABLE TO DO A LOT OF FIRST HAND RESEARCH.
MY SON, THE NATURE BOY— BAH!
IT SOUNDS JUST LOVELY, DEAR.
ALONG WITH THE FIELD WORK, I CAN ALSO TAKE CLASSES IN NATURAL RESOURCE MANAGEMENT AND ENVIORMENTAL STUDIES.
YOU'RE A DISGRACE TO THE WHOLE FAMILY!
THAT SOUNDS VERY INTERESTING, DEAR.
IN APRIL, WE START USING THE CHAINSAW—
NOW YOU'RE TALKING!
WHAT?! YOU'LL POKE YOUR EYE OUT!

HEY DAN! IS ANDY AROUND?
NO, I'M AFRAID HE'S OUT LOOKING FOR AN ADVISOR TO SIGN HIS SCHEDULE.
1-22-86
STILL?
HE'S TRYING TO GET THE HEAD OF THE FORESTRY DEPARTMENT TO DO IT, SINCE THAT'S WHAT HE'S MAJORING IN.
BUT HE'S BEEN GONE ALL DAY.
APPARENTLY, THE GUY'S PRETTY HARD TO TRACK DOWN—
LOOK, I'M DESPERATE— WILL YOU SIGN IT?
HMM, YOU NEED A FOREIGN LANGUAGE.

WHY SHOULD I BE YOUR FACULTY ADVISOR?
BECAUSE, I'M MAJORING IN FORESTRY AND I NEED SOMEONE TO SIGN MY SCHEDULE.
1-23-86
DO YOU THINK I WANT TO WASTE MY TIME WITH SOME KID WHO'S LOOKING FOR AN EASY MAJOR?
IF YOU DON'T FEEL LIKE IT, I'LL JUST GO ASK A DEER INSTEAD—
A DEER?! A DEER AS YOUR FACULTY ADVISOR ARE YOU CRAZY?! DEER ARE THE STUPIDEST ANIMAL IN THE FOREST!
OH, I-I'M SORRY— I DIDN'T KNOW.
"DIDN'T KNOW"—BAH! WHAT DO THEY TEACH YOU KIDS IN SCHOOL THESE DAYS?!
NOT MUCH, MOSTLY WE JUST WATCH TV.

ALL RIGHT, LET'S SAY I AGREE TO BE YOUR FACULTY ADVISOR— WHAT DO I HAVE TO DO?
EVERY SEMESTER I BRING YOU MY SCHEDULE, AND YOU SIGN IT.
REALLY? THAT'S ALL?
YUP, NOW JUST PUT YOUR SIGNATURE ON THE BOTTOM OF THIS ONE.
I GUESS I'LL DO IT—
VERY NICE, I'LL SEE YOU IN THE FALL!
WORK HARD THIS SEMESTER, KID!
THANKS, HAVE A NICE MATING SEASON.

1-24-86
HI, SIR— I'M HERE TO HAND IN MY SCHEDULE!
THAT'S NICE. IT WAS DUE THREE DAYS AGO—
UM—YEAH, WELL I WAS BUSY GETTING MY FACULTY ADVISOR'S SIGNA-TURE—
REALLY? SO THAT'S WHAT THIS LUMP OF DIRT IS? I'D HAVE GUESSED IT WAS A DEER PRINT.
WELL, ACTUALLY SIR, IT'S NOT A DEER—IT'S A MOOSE.
OH.
YOU SHOULDN'T CALL THEM DEER. IT UP-SETS THEM. SEE, MOOSES HATE DEER, THEY DON'T THINK MUCH OF CARIBOU EITHER, BUT—
ANDREW, HAVE YOU BEEN HIT-TING THE EGGNOG AGAIN?

1-28-86
HI DANNY, HOW'S THE BLOOD DRIVE GOING?
NOT SO GOOD. EVERYONE SEEMS TO FIND SOME EXCUSE NOT TO DONATE... HOW ABOUT YOU, ALDO? WILL YOU GIVE BLOOD?
BLOOD
UH - SURE, SURE... JUST LET ME CHECK IT OUT WITH THE LITTLE FELLOWS-
WHAT "LITTLE FELLOWS"?
BLOOD
MY BLOOD CELLS; I'VE GOTTA GET THEIR PERMISSION ... HEY GUYS— HOW'D YOU LIKE TO BE BOTTLED?
WHAT?!
NO WAY!
ARE YOU CRAZY?!
I'M NOT GOING NOWHERE!
BLOOD
WELL, DAN- I'M SORRY BUT—
NEVER MIND.
I'M AFRAID OF NEEDLES!
I'M AFRAID OF NURSES!
I'M AFRAID OF BLOOD!

64

HERE, MR ZECK— JUST FILL OUT THIS FORM AND WAIT FOR THE NURSE OVER THERE TO CALL YOU.
OK.
HEY TOOTS, IS THIS YOUR FIRST DONATION?
EXCUSE ME?! DID YOU SAY SOMETHING?
1-30-86
UM— NO.
AFTER IT'S OVER, YOU WANNA GO SOMEPLACE AND CO-AGULATE?
LIKE HELL! WHAT ARE YOU TRYING TO · PULL?! YOU LITTLE DWARF!
NOTHING! NOTHING! I DIDN'T SAY ANYTHING! THOSE WERE MY BLOOD CELLS! I CAN'T CONTROL THEM!
TALKING BLOOD CELLS?! THAT'S THE WORST LINE I'VE EVER HEARD! NOW SHUT UP, YOU PIG!
OKAY, YOUNG LADY, YOU'RE NEXT—
NO! NO!—WAIT! YOU DON'T UNDERSTAND—
CIAO, BABY—
R-R-R!
SEE YOU IN THE BLOOD BANK, BIG BOY!

WELL, THIS IS IT, BLOOD-GOODBYE. I'LL MISS YOU-
GOODBYE. ALDO!
UM - MR ZECK, YOU CAN GO NOW. THANK YOU FOR DONATING.
OK. BUT BE NICE TO MY BLOOD-KEEP IT WARM-DON'T PUT IT NEAR A CACTUS - IT'S AFRAID OF CACTUSES-
NO CACTUSES!
AH-ER,
-AND DON'T GIVE IT WHEAT GERM-IT HATES WHEAT GERM!
NO WHEAT-GERM!
AYYY!

ON FRIDAY, JAN. 17, 1986 THE E.P.A. THREATENED TO FINE YALE $16,000 FOR FAILING TO INSPECT AND KEEP RECORDS ON THREE ELECTRICAL TRANSFORMERS.
EVERYBODY MAKES MIS-TAKES—
PHYSICAL PLANT
2-3-86
THESE TRANSFORMERS CONTAIN TOXIC PCB'S, THE BIOLOGICAL EFFECTS OF WHICH ARE UNKNOWN.
JUST LEAVE IT ALONE; DON'T EAT IT—
PHYSICAL PLANT
THUSFAR, THE YALE COMMUNITY HAS IGNORED THIS ECOLOGICAL TIME-BOMB, BUT TODAY, SUNDAY, FEB. 2, 1986, THE PROBLEM WILL DEMAND TO BE NOTICED.
IT'LL GO AWAY—
PHYSICAL PLANT
TODAY, IS GROUNDHOG DAY:
R-R-R
AYY!
YALE

WHAT IS THAT HUGE BEAST?
IT'S A BEAR.
NO IT'S NOT. TODAY IS GROUNDHOG'S DAY — IT'S A GROUNDHOG!
R-R-R-
NO WAY! IT'S EIGHT FEET TALL!
IT'S A BEAR.
FOOLS! IT'S A MUTANT GROUNDHOG! IT'S BEEN EXPOSED TO THE PCB'S IN THOSE TRANSFORMERS!
R-R-R-
OKAY, WHAT'S IT DOING?
WELL, IN ORDER TO GROW BIG AND WREAK HAVOC ON MANKIND, A MUTANT NEEDS CONTINUED EXPOSURE TO THE CHEMICALS THAT CREATED IT.
R-R-R-
SO?
SO, IT'S LOOKING FOR MORE PCB'S TO EAT—
ACTUALLY, I'D SETTLE FOR SOME CHILI DOGS.
KEEP AWAY!
2-4-86

HEY FREDDY, WE JUST GOT A CALL FROM THE E.P.A ABOUT THE PCB'S IN OUR ELECTRICAL TRANSFORMERS.
DAMN, NOT AGAIN!
PHYSICAL PLANT
2-5-86
THEY SAY THEY'VE GOT EVIDENCE THAT PROVES WE'VE BEEN NEGLIGENT-
THAT'S RIDICULOUS! WE'VE BEEN INSPECTING THOSE TRANSFORMERS SINCE DAY ONE! THEY'RE TOTALLY SAFE!
PHYSICAL PLANT
THEN HOW DO YOU EXPLAIN THE MUTANT GROUNDHOG?
OH NO!-
PHYSICAL PLANT
FIFTY-SIX CHILI DOGS? ARE YOU KIDDING?!
R-R-R

BOY, THIS IS GREAT! THOSE CHILI DOGS HAVE GIVEN ME THE STRENGTH OF A HUNDRED GROUND-HOGS!
R-R-R
R-R-R
R-R-R
ONE WAY
2-6-86
NOW, I CAN FINALLY VENT MY RAGE ON MANKIND FOR IT'S ECOLOGICAL NEGLIGENCE AND BEFOULMENT OF THE RODENT!
R-R-R
R-R-R
R-R-R
ONE WAY
I'VE GOT THE POWER TO DO ANYTHING! — TO THROW CARS, TO CRUSH BUILDINGS, TO DERAIL TRAINS, —
R-R-R
R-R-R
R-R-R
ONE WAY
I SHOULD PROBABLY GET MYSELF A BIG LEATHER JACKET!
R-R-R
R-R-R
R-R-R
ONE WAY

NEW HAVEN HAS BEEN THROWN INTO CHAOS BY A RAGING MUTANT GROUNDHOG.
I HAVE THE STRENGTH OF TWO HUNDRED AND FIFTY GROUNDHOGS!
R-R-R-
2-10-86
ALL EFFORTS TO SUBDUE THE BEAST HAVE FAILED: THE UNIVERSITY POLICE WERE NO MATCH FOR ITS FURY.
FOOLS!
WHAT FURY!
R-R-R-
EVEN NEW HAVEN'S FINEST COULD NOT CONTAIN ITS WRATH.
FOOLS!
R-R-R-
WHAT WRATH!
BANG!
BANG!
NHPD
FINALLY, LITERARY CRITICS ATTEMPTED TO CONFUSE THE MUTANT...
—THE RELATION IN QUESTION ALSO EXISTS IN THE ENCAPSULATION IN THE POEM OF A LONG CHAIN OF PREVIOUS TEXTS—
R-R-R-
FOOLS!
TEXT
TEXT

WE'RE DOOMED! THE GROUND-HOG'S GOING TO DESTROY US ALL!
WHY, MIKE? COULDN'T THE DECONSTRUCTION-ISTS STOP HIM?
BEWARE! RAGING MUTANT GROUNDHOG!
2-11-86
WELL, FOR A WHILE, THEY HAD HIM PRETTY CONFUSED WITH A CLOSE READING OF "THE GRINCH WHO STOLE CHRISTMAS"; SHOWING THAT "GRINCH" WAS A SYMBOL FOR "GROUNDHOG"—
BEWARE! RAGING MUTANT GROUNDHOG
—BUT THEY ENDED UP GETTING IN A BIG ARGUEMENT ABOUT LITERARY INFLUENCE IN "FAU-ST" WHILE THE GROUNDHOG ATE THEIR TEXTS. NOW HE'S GOING TO DESTROY US!
MIKE, RELAX—
BEWARE! RAGING MUTANT GROUNDHOG
WE'RE DOOMED! WE'RE DOOMED!
IT'S OKAY, I'M SURE THEY'LL FIND SOMEONE WHO CAN SAVE US FROM THE BEAST—
ALL RIGHT, WHERE IS THE LITTLE CRITTER?

OK, PROFESSOR, SHOOT THE BEAST!
I DON'T KNOW IF YOU WANT ME TO DO THAT, I'M REALLY BEGINNING TO HAVE DOUBTS ABOUT USING THIS WEAPON–
R-R-R-
2-12-86
WHAT DO YOU MEAN?!
WELL, IT'S NEVER BEEN TESTED ON AN ECOLOGICAL MUTANT AND I'M NOT SURE IF IT WILL DESTROY HIM OR CAUSE HIM TO GROW IN STATURE AND POWER–
R-R-R-
IT'S A DEATH RAY!! NOW STOP BABBLING AND SHOOT BEFORE HE DESTROYS US ALL!
DON'T SAY I DIDN'T WARN YOU–
R-R-R-
ZAP
BOOM!
R-R-R-
AAAY!
DAMN!
NOW, I HAVE THE STRENGTH OF SEVEN HUNDRED AND EIGHTY GROUNDHOGS!
SABIN

-R-R-R
WE'RE DOOMED! THE GROUNDHOG IS TWENTY FEET TALL AND IT'S YOUR FAULT!
BE QUIET! I THINK I MAY KNOW HOW TO DEFEAT THE MUTANT!
2-13-86
-R-R-R
HOW?
HOW?
WELL, THE GROUNDHOG IS KNOWN TO BE THE MEAN BULLY OF THE RODENT KINGDOM, SO WE NEED TO CREATE A NICE MUTANT WHO WILL FIGHT THE BEAST FOR US!—
-R-R-R
GENTLEMEN, YOU CAN CALL ME A LUNATIC, A MADMAN, A CRAZY OLD PRUNE BRAIN—ANYTHING YOU LIKE! BUT, I SAY THE ONLY THING THAT CAN SAVE MANKIND IS A GIANT SHREW!
-R-R-R
A SHREW?!
LUNATIC!
MADMAN!
CRAZY OLD PRUNE BRAIN!
THEY LAUGHED AT ME AT THE UNIVERSITY!

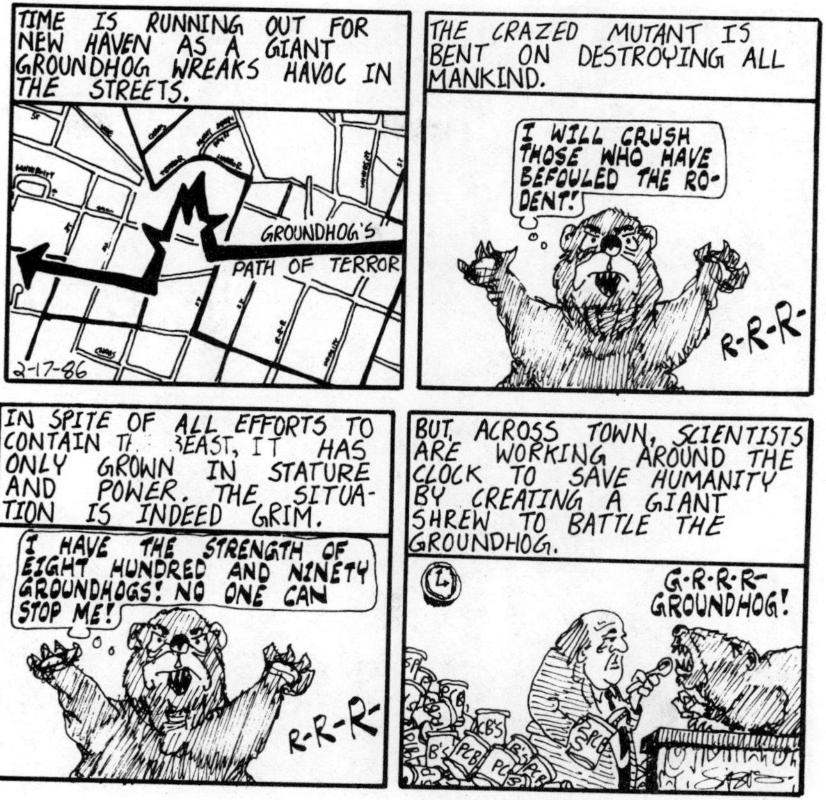
TIME IS RUNNING OUT FOR NEW HAVEN AS A GIANT GROUNDHOG WREAKS HAVOC IN THE STREETS.
GROUNDHOG'S PATH OF TERROR
2-17-86
THE CRAZED MUTANT IS BENT ON DESTROYING ALL MANKIND.
I WILL CRUSH THOSE WHO HAVE BEFOULED THE RODENT!
R-R-R-
IN SPITE OF ALL EFFORTS TO CONTAIN TH BEAST, IT HAS ONLY GROWN IN STATURE AND POWER. THE SITUATION IS INDEED GRIM.
I HAVE THE STRENGTH OF EIGHT HUNDRED AND NINETY GROUNDHOGS! NO ONE CAN STOP ME!
R-R-R-
BUT, ACROSS TOWN, SCIENTISTS ARE WORKING AROUND THE CLOCK TO SAVE HUMANITY BY CREATING A GIANT SHREW TO BATTLE THE GROUNDHOG.
G-R-R-R-GROUNDHOG!
PCB'S

G-R-R-R-GROUNDHOG!
THIS IS IT! GENTLEMEN — I'VE CREATED A MUTANT SHREW, THE NATURAL ENEMY OF THE GROUNDHOG!
2-18-86
I HAVE THE STRENGTH OF TWO HUNDRED SHREWS!
HE'S NOT FULL-SIZED YET, BUT, IF I KEEP FEEDING HIM PCB'S, HE SHOULD BE READY TO FIGHT THE BEAST TOMORROW!
G-R-R-R-GROUNDHOG!
AND IF ANYTHING CAN STOP THE GROUNDHOG, IT'S THE SHREW! HE'S QUICK AND MEAN, WITH SHARP TEETH, POWERFUL CLAWS, AND A KEEN SENSE OF SMELL!
UNFORTUNATELY, HE'S ALSO BLIND—
RATS!

77

78

MANKIND IS REJOICING THAT THE GIANT GROUNDHOG, AFTER DEFEATING THE SHREW, HAS DECIDED TO WALK OUT TO SEA IN SEARCH OF A LAND WHERE MUTANTS CAN LIVE IN PEACE.
R·R·R·
REJOICE! WE ARE SPARED THE FURY OF THE BEAST!
2-21-86
BUT, ALTHOUGH THE GROUNDHOG TERROR HAS ENDED, IT STILL RAISES QUESTIONS FOR MANKIND, SUCH AS: SHOULDN'T WE HAVE MORE RESPECT FOR THE RODENT KINGDOM?
R·R·R·
LET US NOW PRAISE THE NOBLE AND MIGHTY RODENT!
AND WHAT ABOUT OUR RESPONSIBILITY TOWARDS OUR ENVIORMENT? CAN MAN CONTINUE TO FEEL SAFE DUMPING CHEMICALS INTO THE EARTH?
R·R·R·
NO MORE MUTANTS!
FINALLY, WHAT OF THE GROUNDHOG HIMSELF? HOW DOES HE FEEL ABOUT HIS EXPLOITATION AT THE HANDS OF MAN? IS HE BITTER?
CURSE YOU, SABIN STREETER, AND ALL YOUR KIND!
SABIN G.

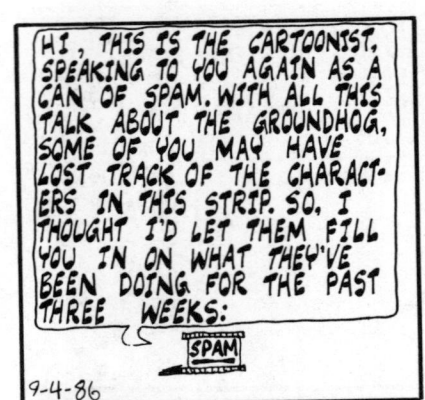

Panel 1: HI, THIS IS THE CARTOONIST, SPEAKING TO YOU AGAIN AS A CAN OF SPAM. WITH ALL THIS TALK ABOUT THE GROUNDHOG, SOME OF YOU MAY HAVE LOST TRACK OF THE CHARACTERS IN THIS STRIP. SO, I THOUGHT I'D LET THEM FILL YOU IN ON WHAT *THEY'VE* BEEN DOING FOR THE PAST THREE WEEKS:

9-4-86

Panel 2: HI, I'VE SPENT THE PAST THREE WEEKS WRITING A PAPER ON EPISTEMOLOGY.

Panel 3: HI, I'VE SPENT THE PAST THREE WEEKS DRINKING EGGNOG AND WATCHING TV.

Panel 4: HI, I'VE SPENT THE PAST THREE WEEKS BUILDING A BRAIN OUT OF CHEESE.

I CAN THINK!

81

82

CONGRESS REJECTED THE TREATY OF VERSAILLES AND WOODROW WILSON DIED A BROKEN MAN.
ALDO, WHAT'S GOING ON IN HERE?
BRAINS BRAINS
9-9-86
THE REPUBLICANS UNDER HARDING OVERTURNED HIS PROGRESSIVE LEGISLATION.
THE CHEESEBRAIN READ ALL THE BOOKS I GOT. NOW, IT KNOWS EVERYTHING ABOUT WOODROW WILSON.
WOW! THAT'S AMAZING!
IT'S A CRIME! IT'S A CRIME, I SAY! WARREN HARDING BETRAYED AMERICA!
YEAH, IT SEEMS TO HAVE THE READING SKILLS AND RETENTION CAPABILITIES OF A REAL HUMAN BRAIN!
DO YOU THINK IT IS MERE COINCIDENCE THAT "HARDING" SPELLED BACKWARDS IS "LUCIFER"?!
THOUGH, IN SOME WAYS, IT'S STILL MADE OF CHEESE.
AGREED.

♫ ♫ OVER THERE! OVER THERE!
ALDO! SOMETHING'S HAPPENED TO THE CHEESEBRAIN!
YEAH, THIS MORNING IT DECIDED IT WAS WOODROW WILSON.
9-10-86
GET ME GENERAL PERSHING!
OH NO!
IT'S BEEN ACTING OUT WILSON'S LIFE RIGHT NOW IT THINKS IT'S 1918 AND IT'S WORRIED ABOUT WORLD WAR ONE.
WE MUST MAKE THE WORLD SAFE FOR DEMOCRACY!
LISTEN YOU STUPID CHEESEBRAIN, WORLD WAR ONE IS OVER! YOU'RE NOT WOODROW WILSON! SO SHUT UP!
WE'LL BE HAVING THE KAISER FOR CHRISTMAS!
ALDO, I'M TURNING IT INTO FONDUE.
RELAX, DAN, IT'S GONNA HAVE A STROKE IN 1919.

UH-OH, LOOKS LIKE THE CHEESEBRAIN HAS TAKEN A DIVE.
SHH! IT JUST ACTED OUT WOODROW WILSON'S DEATH. NOW, IT'S LYING IN STATE.
9-11-86
W. WILSON 1856-1924
OOPS! WHAT CAN I DO?
GO PAY YOUR LAST RESPECTS.
REMEMBER TO SAY SOMETHING NICE.
I'LL TRY.
UM... WOODROW WILSON WAS A GREAT MAN, CHEESEBRAIN– AND YOU DID A GOOD JOB ACTING OUT HIS LIFE... REALLY, I'M SORRY IT HAD TO END—
WAIT! I FORGOT TO DO THE "NEW FREEDOM" SPEECH!

, DAN, AFTER CHEESEBRAIN HED BEING WILSON, IT DECIDED IT WAS PETER FRAMPTON. SO, I HAD TO GET RID OF IT.
ABOUT TIME! I DON'T KNOW WHY YOU KEPT IT SO LONG.
AGAINST BRAINS
9-12-86
IT WAS AN EXPERIMENT.
ALBEIT A STUPID ONE. WHAT DID YOU DO WITH THE CRAZY THING ANYWAY?
AGAINST BRAINS
I GAVE IT AWAY.
YOU'RE KIDDING! WHO WANTED A LUMP OF CHEESE WITH AN IDENTITY CRISIS?!
AGAINST BRAINS
YO! THERE'S SOMETHING WRONG WITH MY SLICE!
IS THERE A COPY OF "FRAMPTON COMES ALIVE!" AROUND HERE?
PIZZA
NAPLES

HEY, DO YOU KIDS KNOW WHERE I CAN FIND SOME NICE BUNNIES ON THIS CAMPUS?
WHY?
WHAT FOR?!
3-3-86
I'D LIKE TO PHOTOGRAPH THEM FOR MY MAGAZINE. WE'RE DOING A SPREAD ON BUNNIES OF THE IVY LEAGUE.
WHAT?!
YOU SICKO! YOU'RE FROM THAT FILTHY MAGAZINE, AREN'T YOU?!
I'M FROM "PET WORLD".
I KNEW IT! WELL, YOU CAN TAKE YOUR SLIMY CAMERAS TO ANOTHER COLLEGE BECAUSE WE WON'T TOLERATE YOUR EXPLOITATION OF WOMEN!
GASP!
ACTUALLY, MA'AM, "PET WORLD" SPECIALIZES IN DOMESTIC ANIMALS. YOU KNOW: DOGS, CATS, FISH—
BUNNIES.
OOPS.

88

OKAY, HERE ARE THE RABBITS WE USE FOR RESEARCH. NOW, WHAT DID YOU SAY YOU WANTED THEM FOR?
I'M LOOKING FOR A NICE BUNNY TO PHOTOGRAPH FOR MY MAGAZINE.
3-5-86
ISN'T THAT EXPLOITIVE?
NAH! "PET WORLD" ONLY PUBLISHES PHOTOGRAPHS THAT CELEBRATE THE BEAUTY OF DOMESTIC ANIMALS — OUR READERS LIKE THAT STUFF. BUT, WE DON'T DO NOTHING DISGUSTING- WE'RE A FAMILY MAGAZINE!
OH WELL, IN THAT CASE, I GUESS THEY'RE ALL NICE BUNNIES.
HEY, THIS ONE'S ESPECIALLY NICE! JUST LOOK AT THOSE LEGS, THOSE PAWS, THOSE EARS—
THAT'S MARYLOU! SHE'S A CUTIE ALL RIGHT-
HOW DO YOU THINK SHE'D LOOK IN LEATHER?
SABAS

OKAY, MARYLOU, WE'D LIKE TO GET A FEELING FOR WHAT MAKES YOU YALE RESEARCH BUNNIES SPECIAL. SO, I'M GONNA ASK YOU A FEW QUESTIONS: FIRST, WHAT ARE YOUR BIG TURN-ONS?
3-6-86
RABBIT FOOD AND CHEWING ON MY CAGE.
THAT'S TOO BLAND! DON'T YOU MEAN, "SLEEPING NAKED ON THE LAWN"? I THOUGHT SO! — NOW, WHAT ARE YOUR BIG TURN-OFFS?
RUNNING AROUND IN MAZES AND SHOCK TESTING.
WHY DON'T WE JUST SAY, "GUYS WHO WANT A COMMITMENT"? ALL RIGHT?— GOOD! SO, WHAT'S YOUR BIGGEST AMBITION IN LIFE?
TO NOT BE DIS-SECTED.
HOW ABOUT, "TO LIVE IT TO THE MAX"?

PET WORLD'S BUNNIES OF THE IVY LEAGUE
AMERICA'S SMARTEST BUNNIES
MARYLOU
YALE UNIVERSITY
"I LIKE TO LIE NAKED ON THE LAWN"
DARTMOUTH COLLEGE
"I LIKE AN OLDER MAN, WHO SMOKES A PIPE"
ALEXIS
COLUMBIA UNIVERSITY
"I FANTASIZE 17 TO 18 HOURS A DAY"
PRISCILLA
BROWN UNIVERSITY
"DO I GET A CREDIT FOR THIS?"
SABIN

92

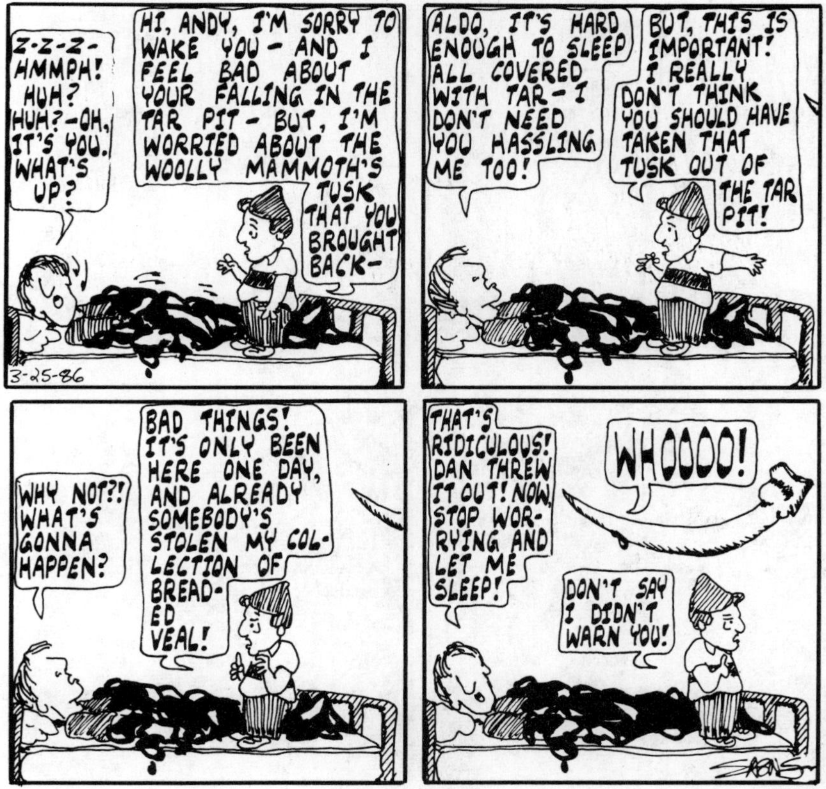
Z-Z-Z-HMMPH! HUH? HUH?-OH, IT'S YOU. WHAT'S UP?
HI, ANDY, I'M SORRY TO WAKE YOU - AND I FEEL BAD ABOUT YOUR FALLING IN THE TAR PIT - BUT, I'M WORRIED ABOUT THE WOOLLY MAMMOTH'S TUSK THAT YOU BROUGHT BACK-
3-25-86
ALDO, IT'S HARD ENOUGH TO SLEEP ALL COVERED WITH TAR - I DON'T NEED YOU HASSLING ME TOO!
BUT, THIS IS IMPORTANT! I REALLY DON'T THINK YOU SHOULD HAVE TAKEN THAT TUSK OUT OF THE TAR PIT!
WHY NOT?! WHAT'S GONNA HAPPEN?
BAD THINGS! IT'S ONLY BEEN HERE ONE DAY, AND ALREADY SOMEBODY'S STOLEN MY COLLECTION OF BREADED VEAL!
THAT'S RIDICULOUS! DAN THREW IT OUT! NOW, STOP WORRYING AND LET ME SLEEP!
WHOOOO!
DON'T SAY I DIDN'T WARN YOU!

94

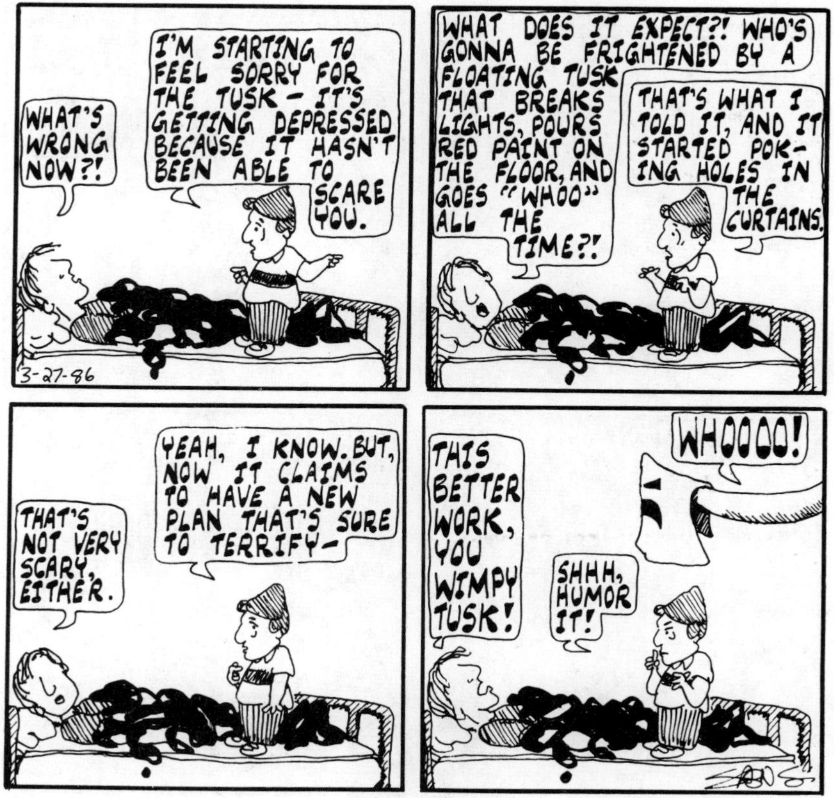
WHAT'S WRONG NOW?!
I'M STARTING TO FEEL SORRY FOR THE TUSK – IT'S GETTING DEPRESSED BECAUSE IT HASN'T BEEN ABLE TO SCARE YOU.
3-27-86
WHAT DOES IT EXPECT?! WHO'S GONNA BE FRIGHTENED BY A FLOATING TUSK THAT BREAKS LIGHTS, POURS RED PAINT ON THE FLOOR, AND GOES "WHOO" ALL THE TIME?!
THAT'S WHAT I TOLD IT, AND IT STARTED POK-ING HOLES IN THE CURTAINS.
THAT'S NOT VERY SCARY, EITHER.
YEAH, I KNOW. BUT, NOW IT CLAIMS TO HAVE A NEW PLAN THAT'S SURE TO TERRIFY–
THIS BETTER WORK, YOU WIMPY TUSK!
WHOOOOO!
SHHH, HUMOR IT!

96

HEY, ANDY - YOU'RE NOT ALL COVERED WITH TAR ANYMORE, WHAT HAPPENED?
THAT WEIRD TUSK SENT US A POSTCARD AND TOLD ME HOW TO GET RID OF IT.
3-31-86
YOU'RE KIDDING-
NOPE, IT ALSO APOLOGIZED FOR TEARING YOUR SHIRT AND TOLD ALDO WHERE HIS BREADED VEAL COLLECTION WAS HIDDEN.
WELL, THAT'S NICE! HOW IS THE TUSK DOING BACK IN ITS PIT?
IT SOUNDS PRETTY HAPPY, I THINK IT REALLY LIKES TAR-
M-M-M-M-M!
WARNING: DO NOT DISTURB THE TUSK!
BY ORDER OF THE CALIFORNIA STATE PARKS COMMISSION

98

THE SHANTY CITY WAS BUILT, AND THE STUDENTS WERE LIVING IN IT TO PROTEST THE UNIVERSITY'S INVESTMENTS IN SOUTH AFRICA.
DIVEST!
DIVEST!
DIVEST!
DIVEST!
WINNIE MANDELA INTERNATIONAL AIRPORT
WINNIE MANDELA CHAMBER OF COMMERCE
WINNIE MANDELA WILDLIFE SANCTUARY
WINNIE MANDELA CITY
4-15-86
BUT, THE PRESIDENT AND TRUSTEES OF THE UNIVERSITY DID NOT LIKE THE CITY.
THOSE ARE VERY UGLY SHANTIES.
WE DON'T LIKE THEM!
SO, ONE MORNING, THE POLICE CAME TO TAKE THE SHANTIES DOWN -
COPS!
COPS!
COPS!
SHANTY!
SHANTY!
SHANTY!
AND ARREST LOTS OF STUDENTS.
DID YOU DO THIS?
SHANTY
UM-
SPEAK UP, BOY!

THE SHANTY CITY HAD BEEN TAKEN DOWN.
SHANTY?
SHANTY?
SHANTY?
4-16-86
ONCE AGAIN, THE PRESIDENT AND TRUSTEES OF THE UNIVERSITY COULD BE HAPPY WITH THE BEAUTY OF THEIR CAMPUS.
IT LOOKS VERY NICE, NOW!
WE'RE GLAD THAT THE UGLY SHANTIES ARE GONE!
BUT, THE STUDENTS WERE STILL DETERMINED TO REMIND THE UNIVERSITY OF THE UGLINESS OF APARTHEID, SO, THEY HELD A RALLY.
DIVEST!
RALLY!
DIVEST!
DIVEST!
GET OUT!
EST NOW!
SOON, SOME STUDENTS DECIDED IT WOULD BE MUCH UGLIER TO PUT ALUMINUM SIDING ON ALL THE UNIVERSITY'S BUILDINGS.
SIDING!
SIDING!
SIDING!
AAAY!
WE HATE ALUMINUM SIDING

Panel 1: THE STUDENTS WERE PUTTING UP ALUMINUM SIDING TO PROTEST APARTHEID.

"DIVEST!" "DIVEST!" "DIVEST!"

4-17-86

Panel 2: BUT, THEY WERE UNAWARE OF A PROVISO WHICH GIVES THE UNIVERSITY ABSOLUTE POWER IN THE FACE OF AN ALUMINUM SIDING THREAT. SO, THEY WERE ARRESTED.

"YOU HAVE VIOLATED THE 'ALUMINUM SIDING PROVISO' AND ARE HEREBY ARRESTED!" "OH NO!"

Panel 3: SOME COMMUNITY LEADERS WERE WORKING WITH THE STUDENTS SO, THEY WERE ALSO ARRESTED.

"YOU HAVE WORKED WITH THE VIOLATORS OF THE 'ALUMINUM SIDING PROVISO' AND ARE HEREBY ARRESTED!" "OH NO!"

Panel 4: THEN, ALL COMMUNITY MEMBERS WHO HAD HELPED THE STUDENTS WERE ARRESTED TOO.

"YOU HAVE SERVED HOT DOGS TO THE VIOLATORS OF THE 'ALUMINUM SIDING PROVISO' AND ARE HEREBY ARRESTED!" "OH NO!"

Everyone involved in the aluminum siding protest was soon arrested. "You have sold aluminum siding to the violators of the 'Aluminum Siding Proviso' and are hereby arrested!" "OH NO!"	**Once more, peace and beauty had returned to the university.** "Look — peace and beauty have returned!" "We're glad that the ugly aluminum siding is gone!"
But, not everyone was so happy; some professors began to wonder what had happened to their classes. "Students?" "Students?" "Students?"	**And some students began to wonder what had happened to their university.** "AAHG!" "AAHG!" "AAHG!" YALE-NEW HAVEN JAIL

102

YERG! ARG! GRCHT!
10-8-86
IS EVERYTHING ALL RIGHT IN THERE, DAN?
NO! I SPEND ALL MY TIME WORKING! I THINK I'M BECOMING A CYBORG!
A WHAT?
A CYBORG. THAT'S A CYBERNETIC UNIT WHICH IS PART HUMAN BEING AND PART MACHINE.
YOU? A MACHINE? I REALLY DOUBT IT.
DON'T BE SO SURE.

SO, WHAT DO YOU THINK NOW?
HEY, YOU REALLY ARE BECOMING A MACHINE!
10-9-86
YEAH, WELL WHY DON'T YOU HELP PUT ME BACK TOGETHER.
IN A MINUTE.
C'MON ANDY! THIS ISN'T FUNNY! CUT IT OUT!
HEE-HEE-HEE-YOU'RE A CYBORG!
BOING-BOING-
BOING-BOING-
RIGHT AWAY, O CYBORG!
DESIST.

DAN, WHAT THE HELL ARE YOU DOING NOW?
JUST BECAUSE I'M BECOMING A MACHINE DOESN'T MEAN I DON'T GET HUNGRY.
RIP!
10-10-86
YEAH, BUT YOU DON'T NEED TO TEAR THE DOOR OFF THE REFRIGERATOR.
CYBORG MUST EAT.
CRASH!
BAM!
WELL, TRY NOT TO THROW FOOD ALL OVER THE KITCHEN.
DAMN! ALL WE HAVE IS CODFISH AND EGGNOG! I CAN'T EAT THIS JUNK!
SLOP! SLOP! SLOP!
C'MON DAN, YOU'RE A CY-BORG! MOVE BEYOND THESE FEEBLE HUMAN DESIRES FOR MEAT AND DRINK.
PERHAPS THE SAR-CASTIC EARTH-MAN WOULD EN-JOY A DEMON-STRATION OF MY HEAT VISION—
CRUNCH CRUNCH CRUNCH

SO DAN, HOW DID YOU BE-COME A CYBORG?
DESIST.
GET AWAY FROM HIM, ANDY!
10-14-86
HUH?
THIS BOOK I GOT: "THE CYBORG WILL SOON DESTROY OUR WAY OF LIFE" SAYS DAN IS BEING TURN-ED INTO A MACHINE BY A HOSTILE ALIEN INTELLI-GENCE.
THAT'S RIDICU-LOUS!
YOU LIE.
NO! IT'S TRUE! HIS ENTIRE BODY IS BEING HONED FOR THE DE-STRUCTION OF HUMANITY!
THAT WOULD EXPLAIN HIS GERM GUN.
NOT TRUE. CYBORG GOOD. CYBORG PLAY PRETTY MUSIC:
WE HAD JOY! WE HAD FUN! WE HAD SEASONS IN THE SUN!
'TIS A CRAFTY ALIEN!

RING-RING-
HELLO?
TELEPHONE.
♫ GOODBYE-GOODBYE-IT'S HARD TO DIE! ♫
10-15-86
DELTA-PRIME DELTA-
DAN, I THINK IT'S FOR YOU-
I KNOW.
OH NO! IT'S THE ALIEN INTELIGENCE CALLING TO GIVE DAN HIS ORDERS!
HIS ORDERS?
OF COURSE, DAN'S BEEN CREATED TO PERFORM A SPECIFIC FUNCTION IN THE ALIEN'S PLAN TO DESTROY HUMANITY. NOW, HE MUST CARRY OUT HIS ERRAND OF HORROR!
CYBORG MUST ELIMINATE ALL GRADUATE STUDENTS.
WELL, IF SOMEBODY'S GOTTA GO, IT MIGHT AS WELL BE THOSE GRAD STUDENTS-
'TIS A WELL-INFORMED ALIEN.

108

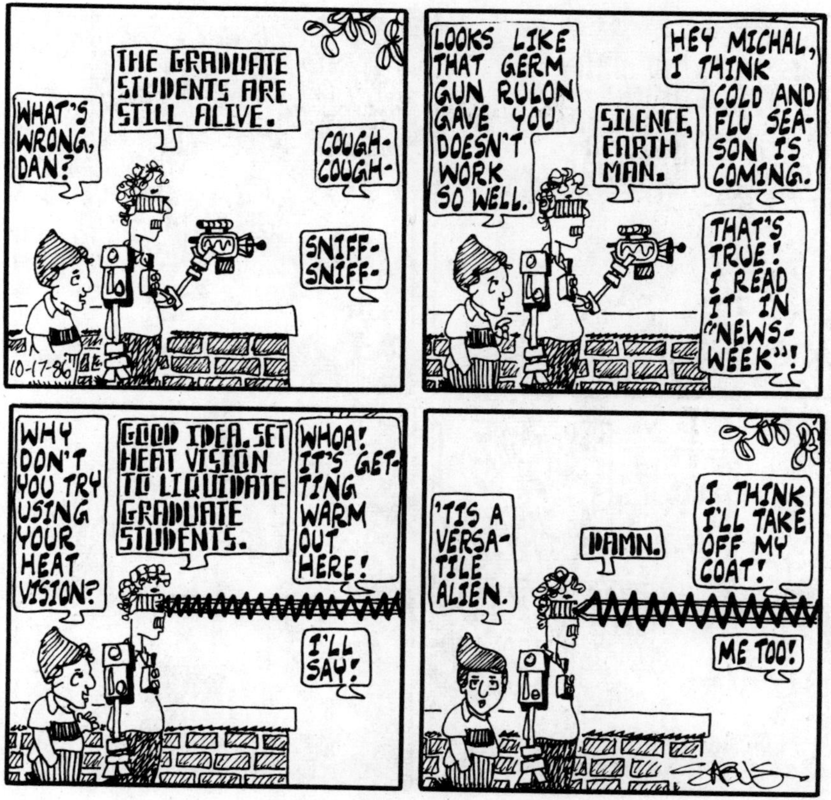
WHAT'S WRONG, DAN?
THE GRADUATE STUDENTS ARE STILL ALIVE.
COUGH-COUGH-
SNIFF-SNIFF-
10-17-86
LOOKS LIKE THAT GERM GUN RULON GAVE YOU DOESN'T WORK SO WELL.
SILENCE, EARTH MAN.
HEY MICHAL, I THINK COLD AND FLU SEASON IS COMING.
THAT'S TRUE! I READ IT IN "NEWSWEEK"!
WHY DON'T YOU TRY USING YOUR HEAT VISION?
GOOD IDEA. SET HEAT VISION TO LIQUIDATE GRADUATE STUDENTS.
WHOA! IT'S GETTING WARM OUT HERE!
I'LL SAY!
'TIS A VERSATILE ALIEN.
DAMN.
I THINK I'LL TAKE OFF MY COAT!
ME TOO!

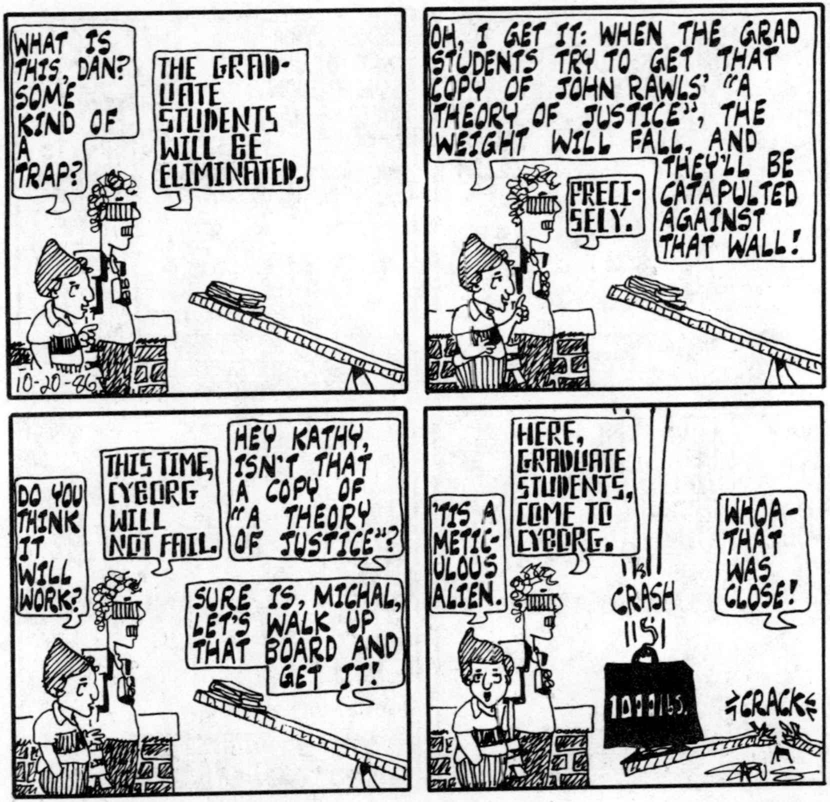
WHAT IS THIS, DAN? SOME KIND OF A TRAP?
THE GRADUATE STUDENTS WILL BE ELIMINATED.
10-20-86
OH, I GET IT: WHEN THE GRAD STUDENTS TRY TO GET THAT COPY OF JOHN RAWLS' "A THEORY OF JUSTICE", THE WEIGHT WILL FALL, AND
PRECISELY.
THEY'LL BE CATAPULTED AGAINST THAT WALL!
DO YOU THINK IT WILL WORK?
THIS TIME, CYBORG WILL NOT FAIL.
HEY KATHY, ISN'T THAT A COPY OF "A THEORY OF JUSTICE"?
SURE IS, MICHAL, LET'S WALK UP THAT BOARD AND GET IT!
'TIS A METICULOUS ALIEN.
HERE, GRADUATE STUDENTS, COME TO CYBORG.
CRASH
1000 LBS.
WHOA-THAT WAS CLOSE!
CRACK

SO, YOU'RE GONNA KILL THE GRAD STU-DENTS WITH THIS MA-CHINE?
IT IS CERTAIN.
GRADULATE
10-21-86
DANNY, PHONE FOR YOU! IT'S PLANET RU-LON AGAIN.
I MUST GO.
WHAT DO YOU THINK THEY WANT WITH HIM NOW?
THEY'RE PROBABLY WONDERING WHY DAN HASN'T BEEN ABLE TO KILL ANY GRAD STU-DENTS.
RULON HAS SPOKEN. CY-BORG IS TO BE DIS-CONTINUED.
WELL, IF SOMEONE'S GOTTA BE DISCON-TINUED, IT MIGHT AS WELL BE YOU.
'TIS AN UNFOR-GIVING ALIEN.

112

113

114

HA-HA-HA-
A FEW MORE
ADJUSTMENTS!
HA-HA-HA-
UM, EXCUSE ME,
I'M STEVE
WILLIAMSON
FROM THE
UNIVERSITY.
7-3-86
WHAT
DO YOU
WANT?!
ARE YOU PROFESSOR ED-
GAR VON DER MÜLLER?
PROPONENT OF THE FIVE
SUN MODEL OF THE
GALAXY, ADVOCATE OF
LUNAR DESTRUC-
TION, AND AU-
THOR OF
"AGAINST
MATTER"?
PER-
HAPS.
ARE YOU THE MAN WHO
DESIGNED AN UNSUCCESS-
FUL DEATH RAY AND A
USELESS NEBULA GENER-
ATOR? THE ONE WHO IS
CURRENTLY WORK-
ING ON AN ANTI-
GRAVITY
HELMET?
ARE YOU
HERE TO
TAKE AWAY
MY GRANT
AGAIN?
I'M A-
FRAID SO.

BUT YOU CAN'T TAKE AWAY MY GRANT! THE ANTI-GRAVITY HELMET IS ALMOST FINISHED!
COME ALONG EDGAR, YOU'VE GOT A HEARING WITH THE FACULTY COMMITTEE NOW.
10-4-86
WHAT FOR?!
TO DECIDE IF YOU'RE FIT TO REMAIN AT THIS UNIVERSITY. BUT, DON'T WORRY, SIMON VON LÜTTEMAN, YOUR OLD CLASSMATE AT THE ACADEMY, IS HEADING THE COMMITTEE.
SO! VON LÜTTEMAN IS BEHIND THIS, EH?! I MIGHT HAVE KNOWN; HE'S ALWAYS HATED ME!
AREN'T YOU BEING PARANOID? THE GOOD PROFESSOR IS A RATIONAL MAN OF SCIENCE.
I KNOW; IN TENTH GRADE I TRIED TO DEMOLECULARIZE HIM.
I'VE OFTEN WONDERED WHY HE CALLS YOU A LUNATIC—

HELLO EDGAR—REMEMBER ME? SIMON VON LÜTTEMAN, YOUR OLD FRIEND? I'D LIKE TO WELCOME YOU TO THIS HEARING; WE'LL BE DECIDING YOUR FATE AT THIS UNIVERSITY—
STILL WORKING FOR THE GOOD OF HUMANITY, EH, SIMON?
EDGAR
DEFENDANT
11-5-86
YOU KNOW EDGAR, BACK AT THE ACADEMY, YOU WERE THE BEST! BUT YOU WASTED YOUR GENIUS BY EMBRACING THE DARK SIDE OF SCIENCE! I FIND THAT SAD.
ME TOO!
EDGAR
DEFENDANT
WELL, NO MATTER. NOW WE'VE GOT YOU FOR MISUSE OF A GRANT, ACADEMIC IMPROPRIETY, NEGLIGENT LABORATORY PRACTICES, AND OCCULTISM!
HMMPH!
EDGAR
DEFENDANT
IF THIS WAS THE 15th CENTURY, WE'D BE BURNING YOU AT THE STAKE—
THOSE WERE GOOD TIMES, WEREN'T THEY?
EDGAR
DEFENDANT

MINUTES FROM THE HEARING OF EDGAR VON DER MÜLLER: 1:00 PM- READING OF THE CHARGES.
-SCIENTIFIC MISCONDUCT, OCCULTISM, ALCHEMY, BLASPHEMY, MISHANDLING OF VOLATILE SUBSTANCES, VOODOO,—
HA-HA-HA-HA-
11-6-86
1:15 PM - QUESTIONING OF THE WITNESSES.
MS. QUIGLEY, YOU WERE THE DEFENDENT'S SIXTH GRADE TEACHER, PLEASE TELL US ABOUT THE YOUNG EDGAR.
OH! SUCH A NICE BOY! QUIET, POLITE, LOVED ELECTRICITY... STILL, HE WAS INSANE-
2:00 PM - QUESTIONING OF VON DER MÜLLER.
NOW, IN 1972, YOU ATTEMPTED TO DESTROY THE MOON, CORRECT?
WHAT MOON?
2:15 PM - VON DER MÜLLER'S DEFENSE AGAINST THE CHARGES.
I DON'T KNOW, THIS IS KIND OF AN UNCONVENTIONAL DEFENSE-
C'MON SIMON, HUMOR THE OLD MAN.
HA-HA-HA-HA!
BLACK HOLE MACHINE

SO, EDGAR, HOW WAS THE HEARING? HAVE YOU FINALLY BEEN EX-PELLED FROM THE SCIENTIFIC COMMUNITY?
HA-HA-HA-HA-
11-7-86
AH, QUITE THE CONTRA-RY! MY GRANT WAS REINSTATED AND ALL THE CHARGES WERE DROPPED.
YOU'RE KID-DING?! WHAT ABOUT THE COMMITTEE?
I LURED THEM INSIDE MY BLACK HOLE MACHINE AND TURNED THEM INTO THIS WHITE DWARF...ALL MY ENEMIES HAVE NOW BEEN SILENCED! NO ONE WILL DARE SCOFF AT ME AGAIN! HA-HA-HA-
WELL, I FOR ONE, HAVE ALWAYS AD-MIRED YOUR WORK!
THAT REMINDS ME WILLIAMSON, I'D LIKE YOU TO TEST MY NEW ANTI-MATTER POD.

HI, MY NAME'S JOE, AND THIS IS MY ORB. I'M A SENIOR, AND FOR THE PAST FOUR YEARS, WHENEVER I'VE BEEN WORRIED, I'D JUST TALK TO MY ORB AND IT WOULD SAY:
JOE, YOU'RE OKAY! YOU'LL GET INTO LAW SCHOOL!
4-21-86
FOR INSTANCE, DURING MY FRESHMAN YEAR, I SPENT MOST OF MY TIME IN THE LIBRARY AND STILL GOT BAD GRADES. SO, I THOUGHT MAYBE I SHOULDN'T BE A HISTORY MAJOR ANYMORE. BUT, I TALKED TO MY ORB, AND IT SAID:
JOE, YOU'RE OKAY! YOU'LL GET INTO LAW SCHOOL!
THEN, IN MY SOPHOMORE YEAR, I DIDN'T GET ANY BETTER AT HISTORY, EVEN THOUGH I SPENT ALL MY TIME WORKING! AND BY THE END OF JUNIOR YEAR I HAD A "C-" AVERAGE AND NO FRIENDS! BUT, I TALKED TO MY ORB, AND IT SAID:
JOE, YOU'RE OKAY! YOU'LL GET INTO LAW SCHOOL!
WELL ORB, GUESS WHO DIDN'T GET INTO LAW SCHOOL?
JOE, YOU'RE A FOOL.
CHENG

HI, MY NAME IS ANNE, AND THIS IS MY ORB. I'M A SENIOR, AND I WOULDN'T HAVE BEEN ABLE TO MAKE IT THROUGH COLLEGE WITHOUT THIS ORB. WHENEVER I GOT NERVOUS ABOUT MY WORK, I'D JUST TALK TO MY ORB, AND IT WOULD SAY:
ANNE, COLLEGE IS NO BIG DEAL— YOU'LL DO JUST FINE!
4-22-86
I SPENT MY FIRST THREE YEARS HERE GETTING TENSE ABOUT READING, NOT BEING ABLE TO SLEEP IF I HAD TO WRITE A PAPER, AND HAVING TANTRUMS DURING EXAMS. BUT, EACH TIME, I'D TALK TO MY ORB, AND IT WOULD CALM ME DOWN BY SAYING:
ANNE, COLLEGE IS NO BIG DEAL— YOU'LL DO JUST FINE!
THEN, THIS YEAR I HAD MORE WORK THAN EVER, PLUS A SENIOR ESSAY! I WAS SO NERVOUS THAT I STARTED HAVING SEIZURES AND FAINTING SPELLS! BUT, I TALKED TO MY ORB, AND IT CALMED ME DOWN BY SAYING:
ANNE, COLLEGE IS NO BIG DEAL— YOU'LL DO JUST FINE!
SO, I FINISHED MY SENIOR ESSAY, AND NOW I'M READY FOR GRADUATE SCHOOL!
ANNE, HAVE YOU LOST YOUR MIND?

HI, MY NAME IS TOM, AND THIS IS MY ORB. I'M A SENIOR AND I NEVER SEEM TO HAVE A RELATIONSHIP WITH ANYONE. BUT, WHENEVER I GET UPSET ABOUT IT, I JUST TALK TO MY ORB, AND IT SAYS:
TOM, DON'T WORRY-YOU'RE SMART, SUAVE, AND SEXY-JUST WAIT FOR THE RIGHT PERSON!
4-23-86
FOR YEARS, I'VE GONE TO PARTIES AND BARS WITHOUT FINDING SOMEONE WHO WANTED TO GET INVOLVED WITH ME. SOMETIMES I'D FEEL LIKE GIVING UP, BUT, I'D TALK TO MY ORB, AND IT WOULD REASSURE ME BY SAYING:
TOM, DON'T WORRY-YOU'RE SMART, SUAVE, AND SEXY-JUST WAIT FOR THE RIGHT PERSON!
THIS YEAR, I STILL DIDN'T HAVE A RELATIONSHIP, AND I COULDN'T EVEN GET A DATE FOR THE PROM! NOW, COLLEGE IS ALMOST OVER AND I'M AFRAID NO ONE WILL EVER GO OUT WITH ME! BUT, I TALKED TO MY ORB, AND IT SAID:
TOM, DON'T WORRY-YOU'RE SMART, SUAVE, AND SEXY-JUST WAIT FOR THE RIGHT PERSON!
YOU KNOW ORB, YOU'RE KIND OF CUTE YOURSELF—
TOM, PUT ME DOWN!
SABINS

HI, MY NAME IS SUE, AND THIS IS MY ORB. I'M A SENIOR, AND WHENEVER I NEEDED THE MOTIVATION TO DO WORK HERE, I'D JUST TALK TO MY ORB, AND IT WOULD SAY:
SUE, THE WORLD IS A JUNGLE— YOU HAVE TO FIGHT TO SURVIVE!
4-24-86
IN THE NAME OF MY WORK, I'VE IGNORED MY FRIENDS, BROKEN UP WITH MY LOVERS, AND STOPPED CALLING MY PARENTS. I'D OCCASIONALLY FEEL LIKE I WAS MISSING OUT ON SOME-THING, BUT THEN I'D TALK TO MY ORB, AND IT WOULD SAY:
SUE, THE WORLD IS A JUNGLE— YOU HAVE TO FIGHT TO SURVIVE!
NOW, I'VE GOT A GREAT JOB! BUT, EVERYBODY CALLS ME A COLD WORKAHOLIC AND I FEEL LIKE I'VE WASTED MY COLLEGE LIFE! SO, I TALKED TO MY ORB, AND IT SAID:
SUE, THE WORLD IS A JUNGLE— YOU HAVE TO FIGHT TO SURVIVE!
AS SOON AS I GRADUATE, I'M HAVING IT TURNED INTO AN ASHTRAY.
AAAY!
SABINS

SIGNET (0451)

MORE BIG LAUGHS

☐ MARMADUKE SOUNDS OFF by Brad Anderson. (136756—$1.95)*
☐ MARMADUKE: TAKE 2 by Brad Anderson. (132874—$1.95)*
☐ "WHERE'S THE KIDS, HERMAN? by Jim Unger. (129229—$1.95)*
☐ "APART FROM A LITTLE DAMPNESS, HERMAN, HOW'S EVERYTHING ELSE?" by Jim Unger. (127811—$1.95)*
☐ "AND YOU WONDER, HERMAN, WHY I NEVER GO TO ITALIAN RESTAURANTS" by Jim Unger. (135458—$1.95)*
☐ "IN ONE OF YOUR MOODS AGAIN, HERMAN?" by Jim Unger. (134958—$1.95)*
☐ "ANY OTHER COMPLAINTS, HERMAN? by Jim Unger. (136322—$1.95)*
☐ "NOW WHAT ARE YOU UP TO, HERMAN?" by Jim Unger. (138236—$1.95)*
☐ IT'S HARD TO BE HIP OVER THIRTY by Judith Viorst. (131320—$1.95)*
☐ PEOPLE & OTHER AGGRAVATIONS by Judith Viorst. (133667—$1.50)*
☐ BORED OF THE RINGS, OR TOLKIEN REVISITED by National Lampoon. (137302—$2.50)*
☐ ENTERING HARTLAND by Rich Torrey. (821459—$3.95)
☐ MORE FUNNY LAWS by Earle and Jim Harvey. (135822—$1.95)*

*Prices slightly higher in Canada

Buy them at your local bookstore or use this convenient coupon for ordering.

NEW AMERICAN LIBRARY
P.O. Box 999, Bergenfield, New Jersey 07621

Please send me the books I have checked above. I am enclosing $_____
(please add $1.00 to this order to cover postage and handling. Send check or money order—no cash or C.O.D.'s. Prices and numbers subject to change without notice.

Name _____

Address _____

City _____ State _____ Zip Code _____

Allow 4-6 weeks for delivery.
This offer is subject to withdrawal without notice.